For my Valentines—David, Becca, and Adam
—L. B. F.

To Jeff, Ginny, Harry, Trudy, and Erica—Je vous aime
—L. A. C.

Text © 2006 by Laurie B. Friedman
Illustrations © 2006 by Lynne Avril Cravath

Carolrhoda Books, Inc.
A division of Lerner Publishing Group
241 First Avenue North
Minneapolis, MN 55401 U.S.A.

Website address: www.lernerbooks.com

Library of Congress Cataloging-in-Publication Data

Friedman, Laurie B.
    Love, Ruby Valentine / by Laurie Friedman ; illustrations by Lynne Avril
Cravath.
        p.   cm.
    Summary: After Ruby Valentine misses her favorite holiday of the year,
her parrot, Lovebird, convinces her that every day is the perfect day to say
"I love you."
    ISBN-13: 978-1-57505-899-3 (alk. paper)
    ISBN-10: 1-57505-899-5 (alk. paper)
    [1. Valentine's Day—Fiction. 2. Love—Fiction. 3. Parrots—Fiction. 4. Stories
in rhyme.] I. Cravath, Lynne Woodcock, ill. II. Title.
    PZ8.3.F9116Lo 2006
    [E]—dc22   2005033956

Manufactured in the United States of America
1 2 3 4 5 6 – JR – 11 10 09 08 07 06

Love, Ruby Valentine

Laurie Friedman

illustrated by Lynne Avril Cravath

 CAROLRHODA BOOKS, INC.   MINNEAPOLIS NEW YORK

Deep in the heart of Heartland,
in a house of oak and pine,
with her feathered friend named Lovebird,
lived Ruby Valentine.

Now Ruby had a favorite day
and Valentine's was it.
According to all who knew her,
this day was a perfect fit.

Ruby loved to say, "I love you,"
and she loved to say, "Be mine,"
and she loved to sign her
hearts and cards . . .

Valentine's was Ruby's chance
to do what she loved best.
As the special day drew closer,
Ruby would not stop to rest.

With **five** days until Valentine's,
Ruby started making cards.
She and Lovebird sprinkled glitter.
They curled ribbons by the yards.

With **four** days down and counting,
Ruby and Lovebird began to bake.
They cut out heart-shaped cookies.
They iced a heart-shaped cake.

They never left the kitchen,
with only **three** days more to go.
Ruby and Lovebird filled up goody bags
and tied each one with a bow.

With just **two** days remaining,
they worked morning, noon, and night,
signing cards and wrapping gifts,
until each package was just right.

With Valentine's **one** day away,
Ruby carefully checked her list.
Then she loaded up her wagon.
No one in Heartland would be missed.

The night before Valentine's Day,
Ruby chose what she would wear.

She tried on her purse and shoes.

She washed and curled her hair.

When everything was in order,
Ruby made a special sign.
It sat high atop her wagon and read . . .

Love, Ruby
Valentine

Tired from all her hard work,
Ruby lay down on her bed.
She hadn't planned to stay long,
just to picture the day ahead.

But when she closed her eyes,
Lovebird scarcely made a peep.
She snuggled up next to Ruby,
and they both fell fast asleep.

They slept right through the morning.

And on into afternoon.

They slept right past the evening.
They never saw the moon.

And when they finally awoke,
Ruby saw with dread the date.
That was when she realized,
she was very, very late!

"I can't believe I missed Valentine's!
Now, I'll have to wait a year
to tell everyone I love them."
Ruby wiped away a tear.

She slowly picked up cards
and started putting gifts away,
when in a squawky voice,
Lovebird said, "Let's go today."

Ruby looked at Lovebird.
"Folks won't like this one bit.
It's the fifteenth, not the fourteenth!
They're sure to pitch a fit."

But Lovebird kept on squawking,
so Ruby made a choice.
"All we can do is try it,"
she said in a tiny voice.

So she straightened up her wagon
and tried hard not to frown.
With Lovebird on her shoulder,
Ruby slowly walked through town.

She delivered cards and candy.

She passed cookies from a tray.

She gave out gifts and goody bags
to all the townspeople that day.

Then she summoned up her courage
and did what she had to do.
"I know I'm so, so late," she cried,
"but I'm so, so sorry too."

What happened next surprised her—
no one seemed to mind!
They just thanked and hugged her
for being sweet and kind.

And that's when Ruby realized
that saying,
"I love you!"
doesn't have to wait 'til Valentine's—
any day will do.

So now she sends out cards all year

that say, **"Will you be mine?"**

And she signs each and every one . . .

Love, Ruby Valentine!